An Odyssean Ode

Nipram Pankhuri

Verses Kindler Publication

Verses Kindler Publication.

Website: www.verseskindlerpublication.com

An Odyssean Ode
By: Nipram Pankhuri
ISBN: 978-93-49532-84-7
1st Edition
Price: INR 199/$13

Disclaimer

An Odyssean Ode is authored by Nipram Pankhuri. The entirety of this published work comprises the original content of the author, who has undertaken diligent efforts in its editing. The characters depicted herein may be fictitious or inspired by real events; however, they are not intended to cause offence or represent any prejudice against any caste or system. Any similarity to the names of actual individuals, locations, or institutions is purely coincidental and serves the narrative. The author bears sole responsibility for the originality of this work; the publisher assumes no liability thereof.

I would like to dedicate this book to my Mother. She was a writer, fashion designer and a wonderful human being. Hope she sees her little daughter following into her footsteps and achieving all the things she wanted for her.

CONTENTS

PREFACE

Time flies and all we are left with moments which become memories. I have seen and been to numerous places and everywhere I go, I end up collecting moments which later turn into memories. Humans are huge admirers of memories because at last everything fades away but memories remain with us for a lifetime.

This collection of short stories is inspired by my travels. I have had the privilege to travel a lot in my early-twenties and the inspiration for this book comes from those travels. I chose to name this book "An Oddysian Ode" because it reflects on my journeys and those journeys are very special to me.

Whenever I am travelling, in the initial days I find myself actively looking for inspiration. However, inspiration is seldom found when I am looking actively for it, it is much later on a random day, in a random moment that I get inspired to write a fictional piece on a completely non-fictional incident.

As a writer, I feel I have poured my time, my creativity and my heart into curating these stories. It is upto my dear readers now whether they like my odyssian ode or not.

I would like to express my gratitude towards my brother, without his support and guidance, I couldn't have become a writer. I would also like to extend a special thanks to my sister-in-law Shreya Sodhia, she has created the amazing graphics for each story. The cover page image is a photograph clicked by me on one of my solo travels.

THE ENCOUNTER

I was walking on the hilly roads of Leh and feeling the chilly wind in my bones even though it was a bright sunny day. I was dressed in a pink winter jacket, blue jeans and a pink beanie cap to keep me warm. When I looked around and saw no sign of a market-looking place, I got this sense that I had lost my way. I looked all around me and all I could see the empty hilly road stretched ahead of me. Looking everywhere made me realise that it was not a very populated street. I sighed and again started walking further on the same road in the hopes of finding someone and asking them about the way to the market.

I had never been good at remembering ways and a terrible cell reception in the area didn't help me either. I was sure that if I didn't ask anyone, I would surely get lost or more lost than I already was and the plan of getting a delicious lunch on the first day of my solo trip to Leh will take a fall. I kept walking in the same direction as before and soon I heard some faint noise which resembled construction noises. As I moved forward, I saw a group of labourers on the other side of the road putting together a new building. I walked towards the group of men and politely asked them if they could tell me the way to the market. All of them first looked at me and then they started looking at each other and one of them said no we don’t know the way. I looked strangely at them thinking how is it possible that they are living here and working but still don't know the way to the market? I again sighed but this time I thought of taking a different way in the hopes of finding a way or a shortcut or anything else. As I walked further uphill in the opposite direction, I heard the sound of a vehicle approaching. The vehicle was moving slowly. I glanced at the vehicle. It was a jeep in which a man who was wearing sunglasses, was looking at me.

The man continued to drive the jeep behind me at a slow speed. When I felt that the jeep had stopped completely, I turned towards the man and asked him,

“Excuse me, can you please tell me the way to the market?” He replied “You are going in the wrong direction.” I uttered a single ohh. Then again I repeated the same question this time and asked “Can you please tell me the way?” He said this time “Yes the market is on the opposite side of the hill.” I could feel myself frowning at the thought of the town square being in the opposite direction of the hill. I thought of walking in that direction then suddenly the man spoke again “I am going in the same direction and I can drop you.”

Without giving it another thought, I climbed in the passenger seat of the stranger’s jeep and the stranger continued to drive the jeep on the same road. I took a glance at him and uttered a thank you to which he didn't say anything. The man was dressed in a winter jacket and he looked like a local of the place. I started to look outside of the window at the tall *deodar* trees which were passing by. The jeep was making a screeching sound on the rocky and dusty road of Leh. After a couple of minutes the man cleared his throat and asked me "So what are you doing alone at this deserted place?"

I spoke in a calm tone "I am here to travel." The guy again inquired "So what do you do? Do you work somewhere?"

I again answered in a polite but stiff manner "No I am a student."

Of course, he had more questions "What are you studying?" My answer came out robotically "I am studying Psychology." He replied with an "Oh you are a Doctor!"

I said no I am not a Doctor, I am going to become a Psychologist. He said it's the same thing. I said no it's different than being a Doctor. So this time the guy said, "I think you are the Doctor of the brain even though you are not a Doctor."

Now having no patience left for arguing, I accepted by saying yeah you can say that I am a doctor of the brain. He had another question ready for me "So can you read people's minds?"

"No, I can't read people's minds" I replied and chuckled a little. Being a Psychology student, I had gotten used to hearing the same question— if I knew how to read people's minds. So now the stranger decided to speak one more time but this time it was not a question, it was a statement that shook me a little "I wish you could read my mind right now."

I looked at the guy now by turning my head in his direction completely to see if he was joking, but his expression rather looked plain and emotionless. I felt a sudden shift in my posture because of his expression. Gladly when I looked ahead, I realised that we were entering the market area and I could see several people around me and it relieved me instantly. The guy now stopped his jeep near a 'bike on rent' shop and spoke in the same plain tone "Next time rent a bike to go to the market."

I instantly climbed off of his jeep and again said thank you as a matter of courtesy. Without uttering any single word, the guy drove off at full speed. Had I known how to read people's minds, I would not have chosen to sit in a stranger's car and several years later I still wonder if was it a good or a bad encounter.

THE DOWNHILL ROAD JOURNEY

The fort was twinkling with night lights and there was a blood-red moon in the sky on the other side of the fort wall. The sun had gone down the horizon and a cold breeze was blowing on the faces of Sonal and Tanu. Although it was only ten minutes ago when Sonal had been a little fascinated with the stories of the leopards and other wild animals who came to drink water from the pond near the fort, she didn't want to experience anything spooky now.

Almost all of the visitors at the fort were gone by the time Sonal and her three friends came down to the parking space of the fort and now it was only these four girls waiting for the jeep to take them back to the base area. The main entrance of the fort was at the ground level. The Mangarh fort was situated on the top of a hill and the small jeeps other than private vehicles were the only mode of transportation to reach to the top of the fort because the entire climb was surrounded by a dense forest area. The forest was green and dense, so naturally, it was a home for some wild animals too.

When the girls came back to the parking space after seeing the beautiful sunset, Sonal immediately had the thought of spending more time at the empty fort but the sky was getting darker and now she waited for the jeep eagerly. The moon was conspicuously a darker shade of red by then and the wind had become colder. All four of the girls were scattered here and there taking pictures and just looking at the beautiful surroundings of where they were. After a while, a faint sound came from the other side of the fort wall to which Sonal got intrigued to see what was in the bushes. While she was peeping down and looking at the other side of the fort wall towards the bushes, suddenly a hand came on her shoulder which made her shriek and jump a little in her place. Sonal turned to see it was Tanu and she was smiling at her. Tanu asked her "What happened babe, why are you looking so pale?"

"I thought I heard something in the bushes" Sonal replied. Tanu's face instantly lit up with excitement "Really? Where?" Sonal pointed towards the bushes. Tanu looked impatiently towards the tall green grass bushes and said "Well I think it might be the leopard which has come to drink water from the pond".

Sonal nodded a little and continued to look in the same direction. When she was certain that nothing was there, she turned only to see that Tanu was looking at her with a weird expression on her face, Sonal asked her "What's wrong?"

"I don't feel good here, I feel like someone's watching us, let's go".

"But how will we go?" Sonal looked around to see that there was no sign of the jeep yet and she also noticed that Meenu and Pihu were not to be seen anywhere. She asked Tanu where are the two of them and she also started to look for them in the other areas of the fort.

While searching for the two girls, Sonal's eyes went up to the red moon in the sky which was now covered with a heap of clouds making the night darker. She had started to feel a little frustrated and the atmosphere at the fort had become very cold. Her eyes went to the fort and it was all dark there, the lights were off and there was only a faint outline of the fort that she could make out in the dark. Sonal gulped the water from the bottle which she was holding in her hands and handed the bottle to Tanu to drink from it.

Soon after that, both of the girls felt that they had slipped into a darkness and there was a complete stillness in the atmosphere around them. No sound was to be heard and no soul was to be seen around the two of them. The jeep which was supposed to take them downhill was still not to be seen anywhere. When Sonal Opened her eyes she realised that she was lying down on the cold hard floor of the fort. Next to her was Tanu who slowly opened her eyes. Sonal looked at her watch, her eyes couldn't believe when she saw the time was 8:30 Pm. She looked at Tanu with a horrified face "Do you know we have been here for one and a half hours, just you and me"?

"What! I thought it's been only 10-15 minutes since we came down from the terrace of the palace" Tanu said.

"No Babe, I think, something has happened to us, look around, there is no one and I feel very strange, it's almost like my head is exploding".

Right after drinking the water from the bottle which was originally Meenu's, the two girls fainted and they were left there lying down on the ground while two pairs of eyes waited excitedly for the leopard to show up. The leopard turned out to be more humane than the actual humans present there. It came to drink the water from the pond and right then, the scent of the humans lying on the ground hit its nose. The leopard recognised the scent of humans and reached near them and seeing the two unconscious harmless girls, at first it decided to feast on them but somehow seeing the serene faces of the two girls shining in that blood-red moonlight, it decided to take a sniff off of them and leave them as they were.

Pihu and Meenu, who were hiding behind the tall walls of the fort, along with the two jeep drivers, felt a huge disappointment when they saw the leopard already returning to its place in the forest. They had a plan in mind which didn't come alive and now they had no other option than to return to the entrance area.

Someone sprinkled water on Sonal and Tanu's faces and they were woken up suddenly. When they regained consciousness, they saw Meenu and Pihu in front of them, both were continuously asking them where they had been and how they had fainted. The two girls were not able to register anything for a couple of minutes and they decided to return to the entrance immediately. In the next few moments, the four girls were returning to the base with the two jeep drivers. The downhill journey was a completely silent one, two girls were thinking about missed opportunities while two were thinking about what had happened to them.

THE HOUSES OF MY CHILDHOOD

When I look back at my childhood, memories always flash in vividness and one thing remains very distinct which is the surroundings of those memories. For instance, when I think about my parents, I always think about my own house in my hometown and my memories there.

My house always felt like solace, calm amidst all the chaos of the world, reflecting an eternal peace. It always seemed like a safe space to express my emotions, and expressions and a space for creation. It also was the *adda* which means a spot (although I hated the term at that time) to have tons of childish fun and not have any worry of the world. My house also seemed like the place that welcomed so many people with open arms. Most of my cousins from my father's side, used to come and stay with us almost all the time. Once my Mum celebrated one of my closest friend's birthday in our house, needless to say, my friend was delighted beyond words.

My house was a two-storey house with a huge terrace on the topmost floor and on the first floor, there was a balcony that was specifically built for me, as I happen to be very fond of balconies. There was an open garden-like space in front of our house in which beautiful flowers grew once. The terrace of my house was another favourite part of my house. From the terrace, we could see the sunset and sunrise every day. Years later when I seek opportunities to see sunsets and sunrises wherever I go, I am reminded of how fortunate I was as a child to see the beauty of nature so close and so effortlessly. Every part of my house is laced with such beautiful memories of my childhood and my teenage years that it almost brings tears to my eyes every time I think about my home.

In my teenage, me and my three friends hung out in my house most of the time. During those years, all four of us had grown very fond of Indian television shows. We used to watch all possible shows which were running on various channels at that time. There were two obstacles in watching the shows—first the lack of electricity and second— my father's disciplined nature. The supply of electricity was irregular in those days, we could only watch the shows when there was the electricity supply and my father was not present in my house. One day, in the middle of afternoon, both the electricity and my father were present, me and my friends were trying to catch up on the episode of our most favourite show, which had aired the previous night and they were showing the repeat telecast during the day. We had kept the volume very low and one of my friends was keeping watch at the door of my bedroom, I was standing very close to the tv to listen to the interesting conversation going on between the two characters. After a couple of minutes, the friend who was keeping watch, shouted, Uncle is coming! I lost my composure, leapt onto the bed, the two friends who were sitting on the bed with books open in front of them jumped on their seats. I grabbed the book from one of them and the friend who was keeping watch joined us hurriedly.

None of us had the courage or the thought to switch off the tv. My father passed through the corridor, saw us studying with our books open on the bed, he didn't say anything and went to his bedroom, to this date, I don't know if my father had seen the tv or not. For days, me and friends kept laughing about the incident. Such were the fun times in the house of my childhood.

My Nani's House was another house where I spent most of my time if I wasn't spending time at my house. The big two-floored house again with a huge terrace and one big compound encircled by a boundary wall consisting of bricks. It was the perfect place for me and my cousins from my mother's side where we shared the innocence of childhood and the dreams of teenage years. In my Nani house, they had a small *pooja* (prayer) room on the first floor. In that *pooja* room, I always wanted to sit in the front beside my *Maama* when everybody sat together to do *pooja.* Listening to my *Maama l*oudly chanting the pooja mantras was something I used to love as a kid.

During the days when I had to live at my Nani house, I used to be so happy that I would get to spend time with my cousins.

But all my cousins were older than me and after reaching a certain age, they stopped playing with me in the open compound of Nani's house where we normally used to play. When I used to ask them why don't they play anymore, they used to tell me that they were all grown up and they couldn't play like little kids. I used to be very disappointed with the fact that once we grow up, we can't play like little kids. I used to tell myself that even after growing up, I would continue to play with my friends. As I am writing this, it all seems like another lifetime, but I do realise that all of this is from eighteen years ago.

Being the youngest among my maternal cousins meant that I was the most adored kid but it also meant that I was the target of the little harmless pranks pulled on me by my cousins. On one such occasion, three of my cousins pranked me with the story of the ghost who according to them lived in the *ducchaati* of the house. There was a small space between the stairs and the terrace of my Nani house. This space was called a *duchhatti.* Once the elders which included my parents, my *Maama, Maami* and my *Nani* had been attending a wedding function at a relative's house. During that time, my cousins had decided to pull a series of pranks on me. One day one of my cousins challenged me to go inside the *duchhatti* and stay there for ten minutes. I was terrified of that small and confined space. I hid there and thought about how a few pairs of eyes would be watching me in the dark. Although nothing was there still I came out sweating from there and in my mind, I had won against the dark faces lurking in the *duchhatti.*

Another prank pulled on me was that I was made to believe that one of my cousins had gotten engaged and soon she was going to get married. She was wearing a thin gold ring on her left hand's ring finger and she blushed a little when she waved that finger in front of my face. I asked each of my cousins if it was true and all of them told me the same story of how she had gotten engaged. The whole day, I kept sulking about how I was not included in the engagement ceremony and when the next day I asked my *Maami* about it, she told me very genuinely that all of it was untrue and I was super mad at my cousins for making a fool of me. My anger vanished when my cousin *Didi* included me in her discussions of her future wedding plans. Sitting on the terrace of the dear old house, we talked about what colour dupattas she'd be wearing and what hairstyles I would be making on her wedding day.

To this date, the house of my childhood friends remains the closest to my heart other than my own house. At that time, their house used to feel tiny compared to the huge number of members living there. There was this room called *baahar waala room* in their house which means the outside room, it was the place where me and my friends shared some memorable times. In the toughest time of my childhood and probably my entire life, that was when my mother passed away, that room and the people inside that room turned out to be the greatest support and strength for me. Just like the winter mist had consumed our entire colony, grief had consumed me. I had given up the ambition of studies and all I did was stare at nothingness for a couple of weeks. Then, one day, one of my friend's father came and talked to me in a firm yet assuring voice. He said to me that I should begin studying and make my mother proud and I shouldn't give up on myself and my studies. Those words gave me the much-needed motivation and I started preparing for my 10th board exams. I passed with excellent grades.

The infinite number of horror movies watched in my friends' house, the uncountable number of laughing riots, the number of the hide and seek games played, all of these things are a blissful part of childhood. There was one game which was very fun during winters, the game where all the kids would hide under the thick blankets called *razai* and one kid would have to identify the others by just looking at them or by touching the blanket, after failing to identify, the kid would be playfully beaten by others. The game always ended messily where all of us would be beating each other under the blankets.

My Mausi's house also was a favourite of mine. Until the time my Mausi's house was a raw mud house, the memories made there are the purest of all the memories. When my parents left town for some work and I had school, and for some reason, I wasn't going to stay at my Nani house, I was dropped off at my Mausi's house. I used to catch my school bus from there and I used to return to the same place from school. It was a different kind of thrill to attend my school from my Mausi's house because it seemed very exciting to catch my school bus from a different place. My Mausi's kids were a lot older than me and spending my days at their place meant that I was going to listen to all the gossip which was not meant to be listened to by little kids like me. I used to feel so happy going to my Mausi's house but then a time came when I stopped loving that house. The cousins grew up and left for college and when I went to their place, it was never the same.

When teenagers grow up, they are not able to connect with their parents and elders. I was always able to connect with my parents, but it was a little difficult for me to connect with my Mausi whenever I went to her home in the absence of my cousins. I felt that I was not at all familiar with their place. Their house seemed more fun, cozy and appealing with my cousins around.

My village house reminds me of the rustling leaves of the huge trees right beside our old house and the dusty roads leading to the vast open fields of the village. My village house is the last house on one end of the dusty roads. That old house has witnessed all the sad and happy parts of the lives of families living in it for years or I can say for centuries. My village house is a traditional Indian-style house with a courtyard in the middle of the house and the rooms are built surrounding the courtyard.

I never liked the village house when the weather was grim. By grim, I mean when it was raining heavily and it was all muddy and drippy all over the house. My Aunts would keep nagging about the house being troublesome. But then winters would come and oh the lovely evenings and the nights of winters. They would bring so much coziness and an overall feeling of warmth even on the chilliest days.

The winter nights are the best when spooky horror stories are narrated and everyone is sitting around the bonfire. The bonfire in my village house is made up of chopped wood placed in a round utensil placed on the ground called *tagadi.* In this weather, a mattress made up of hay seems so cozy and when one sleeps on such a mattress, the sleep is automatically more relaxing. The mornings and afternoons are pretty sunny even in the winter in my village except for a couple of weeks, when there is no sign of sun at all. I think in India, we endure the extremities of the weather because we know that the extreme weather is not going to last forever and soon, there will be a change in the weather.

There is always a hope that better weather will come than the previous one.

In my village during winter, evenings get foggy right after sunset and this fog makes the roads disappear. Nothing remains visible till a certain distance. In that foggy weather, taking a walk feels heavenly. The trees remain still and the birds chirp only when they are returning to their nests and after returning to their homes, the birds also feel like enjoying the laziness and the coziness of the winter evenings.

The beauty of a village in India is that it doesn't change its originality even when the whole world is rapidly changing. The open field which we call *khalihan* in my village remains the open spot where heaps of hays are collected, the milkmen remain the same where the kids of almost every house go early in the morning to fetch milk and the random groups of people still sit together to gossip about the most unimportant things.

Sometimes a house is not just a house, it is a place full of memories that a person wants to keep revisiting.

THE URGENCY

A blue sedan car was running on the NH B-1 of U.P. at full speed and the three young people sitting in the car were loudly singing along to the rap of a Hindi song playing in the music system of the car. Shubhi was travelling from Kanpur to her hometown Kalikapur with two of her cousins to attend the wedding of their elder cousin Sushant. Piyush was driving the car and Raunak was sitting in the back. Shubhi was sitting in the front and she was navigating the map and telling the way. Shubhi felt the need to go to the washroom and said "Piyush Bhaiya, stop the car at the nearest petrol pump, I need to use the washroom."

"Oh man, we had just stopped half an hour ago, you should have used the washroom then" Piyush replied irritatedly.

"Yeah right, I should have peed on the side of the open road just like you two did" Shubhi rolled her eyes.

Raunak and Piyush laughed. Shubhi looked at them with an angry look on her face, Raunak stopped laughing and told Piyush "There is a petrol pump after five kilometres, we can stop there".

"Okay fine" Shubhi replied and looked impatiently outside of the window to spot the petrol pump.

Taking a road trip is always fun and exciting until you are a woman and you need to use the toilet urgently. It may sound like a small problem or not a problem at all to some people because nowadays there are public toilets constructed on the roads and even the petrol pumps provide the facility to use a restroom for both men and women. However, ladies' toilets are most of the time locked on petrol pumps, especially on the highways of Bihar and U.P. and several other states. The infrequent number of women visiting to use the toilets is the reason behind the toilets being locked.

More than fifteen minutes had passed and Shubhi asked Raunak impatiently, " Where is the petrol pump?"

Raunak looked outside of the window and replied "We must be near the petrol pump. I remember in this area, there is a huge petrol pump. Give me the phone, I will look at the map."

About a couple of minutes later, Raunak asked Piyush to stop the car, there was a dimly lit petrol pump on the left side of the road. Shubhi got out of the car in a hurry and looked around to spot the washroom. She couldn't locate the washroom anywhere in the dim light. She saw a staff person sleeping half-sitting on a chair. She went near him and asked in a loud tone,

" Bhaiya, Where is the washroom?"

The person woke up with a jolt, looked at her, rubbed his eyes and pointed towards the backside of the petrol pump and said "There is the washroom madam. "

Piyush had parked the car and him and Raunak came and stood there. Piyush told Shubhi to go and use the restroom while they waited for her there. Shubhi went to the women's washroom, there was a big iron lock placed on the door of the washroom. She sighed and looked at the men's washroom and thought something for a couple of seconds before entering the washroom, but there was a foul smell coming from the washroom which immediately made her feel like throwing up. She covered her nose with her hand and came out of the washroom hastily. She went straight to Raunak and Piyush and spoke in an aggravated tone,

"This women's washroom is also closed like all the others ".

Raunak and Piyush looked at each other and then both of them looked at the staff guy who was on the brink of dozing off again. He looked at them with questioning eyes and realised they were asking about the washroom. He again rubbed his eyes and spoke lazily,

" What? I don't have the keys to the washroom."

Shubhi said, "Come on Bhaiya, there must be a key with you, please open the lock, it's very urgent."

The guy looked at her and straightened up and said " I really don't have a key otherwise I would have opened the lock. Why don't you use the men's toilet?"

Shubhi looked at him and didn't say anything. Piyush quickly went and took a peek into the men's washroom, came back and said,

"You think that's a washroom to be used by women? Even men cannot use such stinking washrooms."

Raunak thought of something and went to the other side of the petrol pump, there was a dense forest that surrounded the area. No lights were to be seen in that area and neither there was a sign of any person there. He looked at the narrow muddy pathway and called Shubhi and Piyush loudly "Shubhi, Piyush Bhaiya, come to this side. I have found a place for Shubhi to go to the washroom."

Shubhi and Piyush went to the place where Raunak was standing, Shubhi saw the dense forest and instantly felt scared. She shook her head and said "No, no, I am not going into this forest. What if a snake bites me or what if there are big ants or worse wild animals, no I will not go here."

Raunak laughed "Nothing will happen Shubhi. We are right here, right Piyush Bhaiya?" He looked at Piyush for his approval. Piyush also thought it was a decent idea considering there was no other option.

Shubhi sighed and switched on the flashlight of her phone and took a few steps into the grass-covered pathway, she stopped after a few steps and looked back at Raunak and Piyush. They urged her to go ahead. Shubhi again took some steps carefully into the forest and she thought of going behind a tall tree which was at a distance of a few feet from her. She started walking a bit faster to reach the tree in a hurry to relieve herself and come back quickly.

There was a rustling of leaves when Shubhi got up and adjusted her dress. She tried to look in the direction of the forest where some noise was coming from. Some footsteps were heard and in the next moment Shubhi's eyes widened.

Raunak was pacing to and fro near their car. It had been more than ten minutes since Shubhi had gone up in the direction of the dense trees. Piyush looked at his watch and then he looked at Raunak and said " Raunak I am getting a bit worried now, it's been ten minutes, what is she doing up there for so long?"

Raunak looked in the direction of the forest, he asked Piyush to call Shubhi on her phone. Piyush dialled Shubhi's number hurriedly on his phone, there was a little ring before the line went busy. "Strange! I think she cut my call" Piyush mumbled.

"Maybe she is coming, that's why she cut your call" Piyush was trying to think rationally.

"You call her number, and I will go and tell the staff to watch our car, if she doesn't come back in five minutes, we'll go and look for her."

When Piyush returned to the spot where they were standing, Raunak's usual chirpiness was missing from his face and he looked perturbed.

"You were not able to contact her"?

"Her phone is switched off" Raunak spoke.

"We should go up there quickly". Piyush also was getting anxious.

The two of them switched the flashlights of their phones on and headed towards the thick forest trees. They scrunched their noses and eyes as the air smelled like cow dung and random insects kept buzzing around their faces. They reached a little up in the forest. There was no sign of Shubhi.

"Piyush Bhaiya, let's try to call her number one more time, maybe now would be reachable" Raunak asked Piyush in a voice that was unsteady and it felt like he would start crying any minute now.

"It is still switched off" Piyush spoke while trying to maintain his composure.

There was a shrill sound of a bird coming from the other side of the forest. Both of the boys had a panicked look on their faces. They started calling out Shubhi's name loudly "Shubhi, Shubhi, where are you?"

No replies came. Now the two of them started running frantically in different directions of the forest calling out Shubhi's name. This went on for another ten minutes. They were tired and they were almost out of breath. Raunak once again called out Shubhi's name but it went in vain. Piyush dialled Shubhi's number one more time, he was disappointed again.

"I think we should call the police now, it's been more than half an hour". Piyush said while moving his phone's flashlight in the dense forest area.

"Yes but before the police arrive, maybe we should search for her with the help of a few people here because I don't know how long it will take the police to reach here" Raunak said.

Piyush went back to the petrol pump and informed the petrol pump staff about Shubhi's disappearance. The petrol pump staff called two friends of his and they all went up to the forest with their flashlights on.

The five men started searching for Shubhi in different directions. It was a dense forest with long and thick trees which made it a very dark forest. They all kept shouting Shubhi's name but no response came from anywhere. The men were now back in one place. One guy expressed his thoughts about the jungle, the other said that the jungle often sheltered wild animals. He also said it is unlikely that any human will be lingering in the woods at the dark hour of the night. This discussion was making Piyush and Raunak more anxious.

"Maybe some wild animal attacked her" the petrol pump staff uttered without a single bit of emotion in his voice.

"How dare you say something like that, you rascal!" Raunak leapt towards him and grabbed his shirt's collar. The other men tried to free his collar from Raunak's grip.

"It is all your fault anyway, a simple thing, a simple thing like a toilet is responsible for all of this. Man, what would it cost you all to keep the ladies toilet unlocked. I don't know where she is and in what condition!" Raunak couldn't stop his tears.

"One of us should have gone with her at least," Piyush said with his head hung low. Raunak came and hugged him and Piyush broke down into tears too. Both the boys were crying when they heard the siren of the police jeep. They ran towards the main road and shouted "We are here, please come to this side."

An inspector along with two constables came into the jungle. The inspector was a tall man with a hint of puffy belly. He was chewing a paan, he looked at the two boys sternly and asked them to tell everything clearly. Raunak narrated the whole incident. The inspector said that they would begin the search for Shubhi, he asked Piyush to send a picture of Shubhi on his phone that he would circulate to everyone in his team. Piyush did as he was told.

"Have you informed your family"? The inspector asked while spitting paan out of his mouth on the ground. "No we haven't informed them yet" Raunak told him.

"Well, then, you should inform them, because it would be most likely a long time before we find your sister.

Both the boys looked at each other with grim expressions.

"Sir, please find her soon, we don't know in what condition she would be in." Piyush folded his hands in front of the inspector with tears in his eyes.

The inspector saw the condition of the boys and he assured them that they would try to find Shubhi as soon as possible. He instructed his team to begin the search for Shubhi. The policemen started searching through the dense forest for the missing girl. Piyush called his father and told him what had happened there sobbingly, his father consoled him and told him that he would be reaching there with some more people and they would find Shubhi together.

Nearly two hours later, Piyush's father joined them along with three men from their family. It was almost dawn when a slightly overweight and tall middle-aged man came to the place where the search operation for Shubhi was taking place. He informed the police that he had heard some muffled noises coming from a small house which was on the other end of the forest. He said that he found the man who lives in that house to be a little creepy and maybe he had something to do with the disappearance of the missing girl.

The inspector and his team accompanied the informer to that house. The house stood on a deserted patch of land at the edge of the forest and it was dimly lit. The inspector asked his team to keep hiding silently behind the big banyan tree and wait for his further instructions. Raunak and Piyush and their family members were there too; they were all looking exhausted.

Almost half an hour later, the wooden latched door of the house opened with a creaking sound which alerted everyone. A lean man with long dishevelled hair who looked in his mid-forties, came out of the door. He looked around suspiciously before bolting the door from outside. He had a plastic bag in his left hand and with his right hand he was carrying a big gallon that looked like it was empty. The man moved towards the unpaved road which further led to another petrol pump on the highway ahead.

The inspector quietly asked two of the policemen to follow the man. The rest of the team waited for a few minutes, then they all went to the house with quick movements. One of the policemen pushed the door of the house open with his foot and when all of the team went inside, they were left shocked to their core. On the other side, the man was arrested by the policemen and was sent to the nearest police station.

Inside the house, near a wall, two young girls were sitting on the raw floor, with their mouths covered with torn pieces of cloth. Both of their hair was dishevelled, one girl had her eyes closed while the other's eyes were wide open. As soon as the girl who was awake saw the policemen approaching, she started making muffled sounds and this woke the other girl up too. "Shubhiiii" Raunak, Piyush and Piyush's father burst in together inside the house.

Raunak sat beside Shubhi, untied her hands and feet and Piyush removed the piece of cloth from her mouth. Both of the boys hugged their sister. All of them were sobbing. Shubhi opened the ties of the other girl too, she was shivering. Shubhi hugged the other girl to calm her down. Raunak and Piyush gave their jackets to each of the girls. They were taken to the main road and from there, they all went to the car.

The other girl told them that her name was Ruchika. She was abducted in the same way Shubhi was abducted. A week ago, she was travelling alone by a bus when she felt the urge to use the restroom but the ladies' toilet was locked and it led her to go to the forest area. It was midnight when the bus had stopped at the petrol pump to get petrol. Ruchika had informed the half-sleeping passenger who was sitting beside her seat that she was going to the washroom. The conductor and the driver of the bus had gotten down from the bus and they were on the other side of the bus smoking and chatting. Nobody saw her going towards the forest. They only realised that Ruchika was missing when the bus was empty after reaching its final stop and they found her luggage unattended in her seat.

Ruchika was unable to contact her family or anyone because the man had snatched her mobile phone and switched it off just like Shubhi's. The police dropped Ruchika to her home in Shrinathpur where her family was ecstatic to see her after a week. They had lost half of their hopes to find her.

Ruchika had told Shubhi that the man didn't harass her physically other than slapping her when she refused to eat or drink. It seemed like the man wanted to do some ritual where he would sacrifice several girls together. He kept talking to himself about becoming a powerful person and he used to collect weird things from the forest and store them in the house.

Shubhi, Raunak and Piyush were accompanied by the police inspector to their home. Piyush's father had not informed others at their home about Shubhi's disappearance because he didn't want everyone to panic. Wedding preparations were going on in full swing in their village house when they reached there. Shubhi was trying to enjoy the functions and act normal with everyone but her mind kept going back to the forest. She was continuously getting flashbacks of how the evil man had attacked her from behind a tree and how he dragged her to that creepy house. When she saw Ruchika there with her hands and legs tied and when

Ruchika saw her, how her lifeless eyes shone with a glint of hope. When both of the girls had tried to scream and make calls for help, the man had stuffed pieces of cloth in their mouths to muffle their cries for help. The whole incident was a nightmare for Shubhi that she wanted to forget desperately.

After a week, all of the wedding functions were over. Once again the trio began their journey back to Kanpur. Shubhi's father was accompanying them this time to ensure their safety. This time Shubhi made sure to not drink water or any liquids so that she wouldn't have to use the washroom. When they passed the ominous petrol pump, Shubhi caught a glimpse of the petrol pump. The ladies' toilet was unlocked this time.

THE HEIST

Once upon a time, there was a king called Raman and his queen named Avanti. The king and the queen lived in their palace in Ramnikpur and they were very happy together. Despite having every kind of wealth, they were deprived of the only happiness which was to have a child of their own. The king and the queen used to spend their quality time in the cellar of their palace. In the cellar, they stored most of their possessions and it was the king's favourite place inside their palace. The king often used to tell the queen that he would love to take his final breaths in the cellar and the queen always used to put her delicate fingers on the lips of the old king to stop him from saying such ominous things. The king loved to lay his head in his queen's lap and dream about having a little kid of their own.

Ramnikpur Kingdom was once known for its wealth and grandeur, however, in the last twenty years, the wealth and their kingdom had taken to a gradual fall. It was said that there was a curse on the kingdom and it was causing its downfall.

Many years ago, there was a heist that took place at Queen Avanti's home in *Ambikapur* when she was a little girl. The robbers had their faces covered with shawls who came to rob the place and among other things, there was a beautiful pearl necklace which was robbed which belonged to the little princess Avanti. That pearl necklace was the little princess's favourite. Princess Avanti had sworn on that day that she would find the robbers and she will take her revenge on them. Years later, the queen had grown up, and she was married to the prince of another kingdom called *Ramnikpur.*

In *Ramnikpur's* cellar, a lot of gold and jewellery were hidden. The Queen did think nothing of them. She was not interested in any of those jewels or gold, but, one day while she was visiting the cellar by herself, she saw a beautiful wooden box with intricate carvings on top of it. The golden latch of the box was glinting from a distance. The box looked familiar to her, she thought of opening it, but one of the guards came to her and told her that the king was calling her. Avanti left the box there and she went from there to see the king.

One day, while Avanti and Raman were walking in their garden, Avanti told king Raman that she saw a beautiful box of jewels and she was intrigued by it, so she thought of opening the box and seeing inside it. The king was puzzled. Avanti had never been the type of woman who was fascinated with jewellery. Upon hearing this, he told her to come along with him and show him the box. The queen went with the king to the cellar and there was the box lying on a big wooden table among all the other boxes. The queen pointed towards the box.

The king took the wooden box in his hands, he opened the golden latch and there it was, a beautiful pearl necklace gleaming in all its glory, which was once Avanti's favourite thing in the whole world. The Queen immediately recognised her pearls but she kept her composure and asked the king where had they bought those pearls from. The king told her that once his father had commenced a heist in a nearby kingdom, and more than half of the jewels in their cellar had belonged to another king and their kingdoms. The Queen asked the king why was there a need to rob other kings and their kingdoms. The king told her they needed to be wealthy and wealth meant that they had power so that nobody could conquer their kingdom.

Queen Avanti was shaken to her core after hearing this, and she decided to take her revenge. She wrote a letter and sent it to her home and called Ambikapur's *mantri* Kishore Singh to Ramnikpur. Once the *mantri* arrived, the queen told him everything. She asked him to organise a fake heist, in which robbers would come and steal all the jewellery and gold from the cellar. This would make the king realise his mistakes of robbing other kingdoms. The *mantri* did as he was told. Little did he know while he was organising all this, the head of a group of real robbers overheard him.

On the day of the heist, Avanti made the king wear his turban and looked at him with a strange look in her eyes. As they were attending the *darbaar*, some *sipahis* came running frantically. They informed the king and everyone that a group of robbers had entered their cellar. Along with *sipahis*, Avanti and King Raman ran towards the cellar. The robbers had already cleared out more than half of the jewellery and a few robbers had fled with the looted gold.

Avanti's eyes went towards one robber, who was going to take the wooden box. She screamed loudly. King Raman followed her gaze and realised that she wanted the box to be saved. He leapt towards the robber immediately but the robber attacked him with his sword swiftly. The king tried to snatch the wooden box from the robber's hands even after being wounded. The box slipped from the robber's hands and it fell onto the ground with a thud. The latch came undone in the next moment. The robber fled away when he saw *sipahis* coming from the front entrance.

King Raman was now bleeding heavily, he was going to fall to the ground. Avanti caught him in her arms. She sat on the ground and made him lay his head on her lap. Tears were continuously flowing from Avanti's eyes as she tried to stop the bleeding from Raman's chest by putting her hand on his chest.

Mantri Kishore Singh arrived in the cellar in a dishevelled state. The scene in front of his eyes was telling the whole story. There was the king taking his final breath in the lap of his beloved queen, the wooden box was lying on the floor and white shiny pearls were scattered all around the king and the queen.

AN ORDINARY EVENING IN SHIMLA

Dhaniram was walking uphill carrying a *jhola* in his hands, his feet had started to hurt and his breathing had become ragged. It was a beautiful yet ordinary evening in Shimla where the sky was decked up in the warm colours of sunset. The birds were doing their usual chirping while returning to their homes. A cool breeze was passing between the hills making the summer evening more pleasant. Dhaniram was in a hurry to reach to the other side of the Kaali hills. In between his hurry and the sound of his heavy breathing, he could not hear the horn of the small car which was coming down the road behind him. Soon the car reached near him and the man at the steering wheel rolled his windows down.

"Mistri Jee, are you alright?"

Dhaniram turned his head and seeing a familiar face he smiled "Yes, yes, I am alright Singh *sahab,* you all please carry on."

The little children sitting in the backseat of the car waved and shouted in their cute childish voices, "Bye-bye, *Mistri* Uncle!"

"Bye-bye kids", Dhaniram waved at them too. He looked at the little shop of tea and snacks on the bend of the hill and walked towards the shop. There were a couple of people at the shop talking among themselves.

Dhaniram took his *beedi* out of his cotton trouser's pocket and lit the *beedi* up with the lighter hanging with a thread like rope at the shop's counter. He took a sip and looked at the beautiful view of the hills and the pretty town with a few lights on. It was an evening just like the other evenings in Shimla where tourists came and went to and from Shimla every day and the locals continued to go on with their daily routine lives. But for Dhaniram, it was a special evening because he was leaving for his hometown the next morning on the seven am bus which took off from the town centre's bus stand every day. He continued taking sips from his *beedi* and thought to himself "I will miss this town, these hills and these people."

Getting up from his place, Dhaniram started walking again towards his destination. Soon he reached a house at the end of the downhill road and he stopped. He sighed looking up towards the house. The house was nothing short of a palace and it was surrounded by tall trees and plants making it stand out more. He glanced at the road up and down to see whether someone was looking at him or not. After being sure that nobody was watching him, he carefully entered through the wooden back door of the house. He kept taking small soundless steps towards the orchard where all kinds of plants and trees were growing.

He approached a big mango tree, placed his *jhola* on the ground, took out a medium-sized shovel from his *jhola* and started to dig the soil as quietly as possible. He kept digging for about twenty minutes and as the pit became deeper, he put aside his shovel and started to remove the soil from the ground with his hands. Now excited with anticipation, his breathing became faster and soon he realised that the pit he had dug was empty. A cloud of disappointment and sadness covered Dhaniram after finding out that the box he had hidden in the orchard of this big house was not there. After sitting there for a while, Dhaniram took his shovel, kept it inside his *jhola,* dusted the soil off his trousers and got up to leave from there but froze in his place when he heard a voice calling his name.

"Dhani Uncle, wait, are you looking for this?" A young man reached near him and showed him the small tin box he was carrying in his hands. White lilies were painted on the top part of the box and the bottom part of the tin box had begun to rust.

Dhaniram was completely flustered with this sudden reappearance of his lost treasure but he couldn't say anything to the young man standing in front of him. The last time Dhaniram saw this young man named Kabir, he was a little boy who was the only child of the owner of this big house. Little Kabir used to follow his Dhani uncle everywhere all the time. His non-stop questioning about building a house used to make Dhani's day and he used to answer all of his questions with a smile. Now the little boy was grown up into a tall man with a thin moustache and sharp features. The childish voice was replaced by a heavy and manly voice.

"It's okay Dhani Uncle, I know this box is yours. I saw you hiding it in our orchard thirty years ago when you were building our house."

"Why have you kept it with yourself all these years and why are you returning it to me?" Dhaniram's eyes were full of questions.

"You remember Dhani Uncle, how I used to trouble you with all those questions about building a house when you were working at our house and you were always patient with me. You always explained everything to me calmly. It's because of those three months, I decided to become an architect and today I am a successful architect. If you weren't there to give water to my curious seeds, I would not have chosen architecture to study and I am forever grateful to you for your patience and kindness."

Kabir handed the small tin box to Dhaniram and when he held that small box, his eyes welled up. He looked at Kabir with a grateful smile and thanked him. Kabir touched his feet to which Dhaniram was startled at first but gave him blessings that came out from his mouth but those blessings were actually coming out straight from Dhani's heart.

On his way back from Kabir's house, Dhaniram was lost in the thoughts about how he had found a gold-filled big box with two other men when they were doing the digging work at the new graveyard of Shimla. Since it was a graveyard where the men had found the little treasure, they had decided to divide the gold among themselves. Dhaniram had decided to bury his share of gold in the soil of the big mansion he was building because he had no other place to keep the gold safe and he couldn't trust anyone to keep the box with them.

After burying the small box, Dhaniram decided that he would take out the box at the time when he would finally return to his hometown. He would be a hero to his family when he would show that he had brought such treasure for them. But thirty years passed and Dhani was not able to leave the place due to the constant work and now finally he had the treasure with him. Dhaniram had come across all kinds of people in thirty years in Shimla, some had been kind to him, some had not been kind to him. But no one had came across as a dishonest person, and this is what Dhaniram admired the most about these people in the hills.

The next morning, Dhaniram was on the bus which was leaving Shimla and he was leaving this place forever. He opened the tin box and took out the small potli and opened it, he found a good amount of cash along with his gold and there was a small note in which it was written "Thank you" in Hindi. The bus was moving ahead and Dhaniram was occupied with his thoughts about how he had this box filled with gold and cash in his hands yet the gesture of the boy was the most precious thing he was carrying with him in his heart.

TAMANG

Often when we think about soul searching and reconnecting with our true selves, we march towards the hills because we think that's where the peace and quiet lie. That is why I also decided to reach the mountains of Himachal Pradesh when I was feeling highly frustrated with my job and myself. Lately I had become irritable and I wasn't feeling satisfied with my work, my lifestyle and when I looked into a mirror, the person I saw didn't feel like myself anymore. I had taken a week's leave and another week to work from home and presently I was standing on the side of a main road in a small valley of Himachal Pradesh.

I heard a voice calling someone. "Aye Tamang! Come here and serve the tea." I turned to see where was this sound coming from and saw a cute looking girl with a lovely smile going to give a cup of tea to the person. The girl was dressed in a black overcoat which had a belt in the front and snow boots. She had distinct *pahadi* features and she looked like she could be in her late twenties.

After giving the tea to the old man, the girl went inside the small tea shop which was standing on the other side of the road. She was making tea in the shop. I kept looking at her now and then along with smoking my cigarette. I was standing at a small distance from where I could see her hands rhythmically working at the gas stove, she was working with dedication making tea and maggie with a peaceful expression on her face. I observed her and the shop for some time and then I went back inside the hotel where I was staying.

The next day, I was taking a stroll around my hotel and I was just looking at the mountains. I thought to myself, "How do these mountains look so peaceful all the time, how do they endure everything so calmly, the havocs created by nature, the atrocities brought up by humans?" All these thoughts were running in my mind and while thinking all this, I reached the small tea shop.

I went inside the shop and looked around, it was a very small shop with some packets of chips and biscuits hung on a wall, and there were a couple of small tables and benches set up for sitting. I quietly sat on a bench. The same girl was working there and I thought that her name was Tamang because I had overheard the guy calling her the other day. I looked at her for a couple of seconds and when she didn't look at me, I stood up and said, "Hi, can I get a cup of tea?" She looked at me and smiled and replied with a small "Sure."

I tapped on the table with my fingers where I was sitting and she looked at me while making the tea and smiled a little. I asked her in a loud voice "Do you work here alone?"

She brought a cup of tea and placed it gently on my table and replied "No, my uncle also helps me with the work."

"Is there any other place to eat around here?" It was my second attempt at making a conversation. She looked up at me in bewilderment. I clarified that I was asking for other kinds of food and not another place to eat maggie and momos which they were already selling at their shop. She told me there was a newly opened restaurant up on the main road which I could try. A couple of cars stopped at the shop and some people came inside and they ordered a few things, and once again Tamang got busy with preparing food with her usual zeal.

I picked up my cup from the table and sipped the steaming tea. After finishing the tea, I stood up and walked towards her and asked "How much for the tea?"

She said, "Twenty rupees."

I took out a twenty rupees note from my wallet and gave it to her. She kept the money in the small drawer of the table.I asked her again "Is your name Tamang?"

She smiled and said " No, my name is Roshni, my surname is Tamang."

I felt a little stupid and said "Oh okay, I thought your name was Tamang."

She looked at me and asked "What is your name?"

I told her my name.

The next morning, I took a bath with an icy cold water in the bathroom of my hotel because the geyser was not working in my bathroom. After I got dressed, I went to the balcony of my room. The balcony was a road facing one, I could see Tamang's little shop from there. There was a white van parked outside of the shop, her old Uncle was unloading the things from the van and Tamang was carrying them inside. I came back into the room, grabbed my phone, wallet and a book and climbed down the stairs of my hotel and reached her shop. She looked at me and smiled, I asked for a cup of *chai* and *maggie.* This went on for a couple of days. Slowly a friendship formed between me and Tamang.

The next week I asked Tamang if there was a place in the valley where the usual crowd didn't reach. She told me she knew a place. I requested her to show it to me. The next day we were sitting on a rock near the shore of the river on the opposite side of the valley. It took us a trek, a muddy way and half an hour to reach the spot. It was a very peaceful place, the trees were swaying a little with the breeze and the river was flowing with a steady flow. I threw a stone in the river and asked her,

"Don't you want to leave from here ever?"

"Why would I want to leave from here when I am completely happy being here?" she looked at me with her cat shaped light green eyes.

"Well, I think you can be happy at any other place. How can you know that you can't be happy being at another place if you haven't been to any other place?"

"I haven't but I know someone who went to a different place to be happy because she couldn't be happy here and you know what happened to her?"

I looked at her with puzzled eyes and she took out her mobile phone from the pocket of her jacket and opened a photo of a pretty looking girl and showed it to me.

The girl in the picture looked like she must be in her mid twenties. She had brown and golden streaks in her straight hair and her eyes were cat shaped. She looked like someone related to Tamang because they had similar facial features.

I took a look at the picture and asked her "What do you mean? She looks completely normal and happy to me."

"Oh well, that is because you don't know her, I knew her since she was born and the girl I used to admire and adore the most has become so unrecognisable to me." She took a little pause before continuing.

"You know it is the saddest thing that can ever happen to a person, when they become unrecognisable to their own loved ones."

I realised that it could be the truth of my own life. I wanted to hear the complete story from Tamang's mouth.

She spoke calmly "She is my little sister. Her name is Kajal, since we were little, she had been obsessed with movies and tv shows. She always used to say that when she would grow up, she will become a tv star. She used to dance with such energy and it was always a lovely sight to see her dancing her heart out."

I watched Tamang tell the story about her little sister, her eyes gleamed while she talked about her sister.

"After completing her school studies, Kajal left for Delhi for college. She was determined to get into the field of acting, there she did theatre for a couple of months. When she was in the second year of her college, she got an offer to play a small part in a tv serial. She went to Mumbai and she kept getting offers for roles one by one, soon she was a famous tv actor."

Tamang sighed "You know , she came to our village after three years last year. Other than her appearance, her personality is also completely changed. The girl who used to be happy with even the smallest things, doesn't appreciate the good things in her life anymore. She mocked our ways of working, the simple pahadi lifestyle doesn't suit her anymore, she doesn't even like her favourite food *thukpa* anymore."

"Yeah but you know, it happens when people leave their hometown, they change, their habits change, it is quite normal." I put my perspective in front of her.

"Yeah, changing habits, appearances are not the problem, but changing the person once you used to be is the problem." Roshni Tamang said and I agreed with her. After talking to Tamang, I went back to my hotel. Her words kept replaying in my head. I was beginning to think that I had changed in ways that wasn't me.

I had indulged in the small town jokes my colleagues used to make on other colleagues who also came from small towns like me. Being from Bareilly I had started to tell people that I was from Bangalore. Changing habits and lifestyle isn't a bad thing but deep down I knew that I had started to feel ashamed of belonging from a small town. The worst part was that when my parents were visiting me from Bareilly, I didn't make them meet any of my Bangalorean friends because I was afraid of getting embarrassed because of my own parents.

All these things kept playing in my head till the next morning. My eyes were swollen in the morning when I looked at my image in the mirror. I knew I had been wrong, if I couldn't be proud of my home town then at least I shouldn't be ashamed of it. The houses may be small in small towns but the hearts of the people living in them are bigger. Maybe one day I will be proud of my hometown. I often wondered, how do the people here not want to leave ever and what happens to those who choose to leave. Maybe I knew the answer now.

A HORROR STORY

Ashmita was travelling to Jodhpur for the first time, and her friend Isha was accompanying her. It was Ashmita's twenty fifth birthday and she had come to Jodhpur to celebrate. On Ashmita's birthday, Ashmita and Isha visited the majestic fort of Jodhpur and had lunch at a small Rajasthani restaurant. The day after Ashmita's birthday, her friend Isha left for her hometown leaving Ashmita alone for the next four days.

Ashmita had always been a fan of horror places and she was the one who always urged her friends to go to see spooky places in Nagpur when she was there for her college studies. However, other than seeing places that had some slight spookiness, she had not encountered anything that could be considered spooky.

Ever since Ashmita had come to Jodhpur, she kept feeling a chill running in her body and she was not sure whether it was the weather or something else which was making her feel cold. As long as her friend Isha was with her, she tried to avoid this feeling and succeeded a little but since the time her friend left, she couldn't ignore this feeling anymore. She wanted to understand the reason behind this feeling but decided not to tell anyone about this feeling. She was staying in a traveller's hostel and two days after her friend left, she decided to go for lunch alone one afternoon.

The restaurant was a ten-minute walk away from her stay. After grabbing lunch, Ashmita was returning to her stay. The narrow lanes of Jodhpur looked emptier than usual and there was a chilliness in the wind despite it being a sunny day. The blue houses of Jodhpur were always fascinating to look at. The traditional Rajasthani gates and windows painted in vivid colours of those houses were more beautiful than the houses. While Ashmita was passing through a lane, she passed through a small dull house, its huge gate suddenly opened with a creaking sound and it felt like someone was looking at her. She tried to look inside but no one was there. The house looked older than the other houses on that lane. She kept walking.

After a couple of minutes, Ashmita felt like someone was following her but when she turned to see behind her, no one was there. She felt strange and a bit confused about feeling like someone was behind her. Now her feet increased their pace on their own and her breathing had also become rapid. In the middle of the afternoon, she had never felt scared like this in her life before and her gut was telling her to reach to her stay as soon as she could. In five minutes, Ashmita reached her stay and went upstairs to her room gasping for air and breathing heavily. She lay down on her bed and took some heavy breaths and picked up her mobile phone to call someone but then she sighed and kept the phone back on the bed. She closed her eyes for a few moments and she thought to herself that it must be her mind imagining scenarios which are not real. The next two days passed quickly, Ashmita had nearly forgotten about the incident in these two days.

One night, Ashmita went for dinner by herself. While going to the restaurant, she passed through the same lane where she had felt the presence of someone the other day. At first, she felt sceptical about passing through the same lane, but as she passed through the blue lane, she didn't see or feel anything strange this time. She was relieved and she went to the restaurant and had her dinner pleasantly. When Ashmita was done having her happy meal which was simply *dal, chawal* and *aaloo ki sabji*, she began walking back to her stay.

There was no moon in the sky on that night making it a completely dark night. The pleasant weather had suddenly turned into a chilly but stiff weather. Ashmita felt like the short journey back to the her stay suddenly started to seem longer than before. Her fear had resurfaced. Now she was feeling like she had made a mistake by going for dinner by herself on such a dark night. Again she passed through the same empty lane where the old house stood and the pretty but the old door had opened. Ashmita wanted to go by the house as fast as she could, but in a blurry moment when she reached near the house, someone pulled her hand tightly and dragged her inside the old scary house. For the next couple of minutes, Ashmita felt like she was losing consciousness, her head felt heavy and she could not see anything clearly but she heard a little kid's voice giggling at a distance.

After her vision and mind cleared, Ashmita saw someone standing at a few feet's distance. It was a small child wearing a small Rajasthani turban and outfit and the child smiled at her. She smiled back at him. Ashmita looked around, she was standing in a traditional Rajasthani house, there was a courtyard in the middle of the house and a few rooms surrounded the courtyard. There were four lamps hanging in the four corners of the house. A little breeze was blowing which made the curtains of the house sway softly. In another corner of the house, the little child was standing. Ashmita called the child "Babu, come here."

The little child giggled and ran away. Ashmita followed the kid, the kid went inside a dark room and giggled. Ashmita again called for the kid, the kid kept running from here to there without saying anything. After a while, Ashmita got tired of this running and chasing, she sat in the courtyard to catch her breath. This time the kid came behind her suddenly and pulled on her dress making her jump in her place. Ashmita asked the kid "What do you want Babu?"

The kid again giggled and ran up the stairs which led to the terrace of the house and she felt frustrated and stormed towards the main gate of the house to leave from there.

When she tried to open the door, the huge door got shut with a loud thud. Ashmita was frightened now. She felt like she was trapped inside that old and creepy house. The little kid was nowhere to be seen now and Ashmita looked at her mobile phone to call someone but there was no network in her mobile phone. She felt very uneasy and her throat felt dry. She took out her water bottle from her bag and drank a little water from it. While she was drinking the water, she felt like she was being watched by a pair of green eyes in the dark.

Ashmita's breath got stuck in her throat when she saw there was a small but wild pig staring at her, its nostrils flaring at her. Ashmita screamed loudly and ran towards the other corner of the house, the little pig took a leap towards her from those stairs, Ashmita felt like she was going to die. She screamed loudly once again and closed her eyes because of fear. The little pig came near her, circled her once and then ran up the stairs.

When Ashmita opened her eyes, her head felt lighter than before and she saw the main entrance of the house was open now. She regained her composure hastily and ran outside of the house. After she reached outside and stood in the narrow lane, she heard the same giggling sound, she looked up and saw the same little child waving bye to her. She whispered under her breath "Bye Babu" and left from there.

MANJARI

A group of five friends were sitting on the terrace of the *Serendipity* traveller's hostel in Pushkar. The sky was darker and cloudier as compared to the previous nights. There were only a couple of guests other than the group of friends who were sitting on the terrace at that time. The friends were just looking at the serene lake view. *Serendipity* was located at a beautiful location in Pushkar. Shriya, Neeti, Rishabh, Shantanu and Faizal were the names of the friends who had met in the hostel and had become friends. Shriya looked at Neeti and said, "You know it is *Amavasya t*onight and you know what that means."

Neeti looked at the sky. Her face turned white in an instant and she looked at her new friend with a horrified expression. Long-haired and a lean built Shantanu lit his cigarette with a lighter, put the lighter back on the table and blew a puff out of his mouth and said,

"Shriya, why are you teasing this poor girl? She got so scared the other day and we decided that we would not talk about ghosts and spirits again."

Shriya and others laughed while Neeti made a face at them. Soon they all got busy talking about other subjects of interest. This group of friends was newly found in the hostel where they were staying, being of almost the same age, they all had formed a fun bond with each other. Three days ago, when Neeti had become friends with Shantanu, very soon their conversations diverted from normal topics to the ever-interesting topic of spirits and ghosts. Neeti listened to all of the stories narrated by Shantanu, Rishabh and Faizal with a keen interest and she was the one who kept asking for more stories.

However, when it was time for her to go to bed, she was terrified because all of the stories were being replayed in her mind. Upon reaching her room, she was scared of every little object that was placed in the room, and as soon as she turned off the lights of her room, she felt like someone was standing by her bed and watching her just like in one of Shantanu's stories. She leapt off the bed in a second, took her phone and ran for her life, screaming at the top of her lungs. She reached the common room where her friends were still sitting and chatting, they saw her coming in that state and all of them were concerned for her.

Neeti was shivering because of fear, she hugged Shriya tightly, Shriya consoled her and asked her what happened "There was a woman standing by my bed when I turned off the lights, so I got very scared and ran."

"Oh, man, Neeti, you are so *fattu*" Shantanu began laughing. All of them started laughing.

Rishabh said, "Neeti, there is nothing in your room, you have listened to the stories earlier and now your mind is making up things that aren't there."

"Come sit for a while with us and drink this water" Faizal handed her a glass of water. Neeti gulped down the water quickly and they all sat in a circle. Neeti was still clutching Shriya's hands tightly.

During the next two days, all of them kept teasing Neeti about the incident. The weekend was over and it was a Monday night which was also the night of *Amavasya* (new moon). Past midnight, the other guests went to sleep leaving only the group with their constant chatter and banter.

Rishabh looked at the sky, stretched his body and said "You know I really wish to encounter a spirit or a ghost someday, what fun it will be."

Neeti looked at him with a horrified expression and replied "Why are you raising these topics again, Rishabh? Please, I am scared."

"Oh come on Neeti, nothing is here to be scared about, be brave, you have traveled solo to so many places, has anything like this ever happened to you?" Rishabh tried to console Neeti.

Neeti shook her head in no and looked at Shriya who was taking a sip of a half-finished cigarette, she blew out a puff and passed the cigarette to Faizal. She looked at Neeti and spoke lovingly,

"Babe you know, Rishabh is right, you are a brave girl, and we are only talking about ghosts and spirits and it's not like we are inviting anyone through Ouija boards like they do in horror movies."

Neeti smiled half heartedly and said that she was going to sit on the swing and listen to music for some time.

When Neeti was gone, again Rishabh said "But you know guys, I really wish to encounter a ghost someday."

Shantanu made a face and said, "You know if you want to see a ghost so desperately you might actually see one day."

Neeti was swinging on the swing slowly and music was playing in her ears as she had earplugs in her ears. A girl wearing a white t-shirt and blue jeans came on the terrace, she had a water bottle in her hand, and she sat in one of the high chairs which were placed near the boundary of the terrace overlooking the lake. The girl smiled at Neeti but Neeti was engrossed in her music so the girl didn't do anything further. She then looked at the group and plopped down from the high chair and approached them in a friendly manner. She asked Shriya in a polite tone "Can I join you guys if you all don't mind?"

Shriya smiled and said "Yeah sure why not? Sit. Are you travelling solo?"

The new girl pulled a chair and sat beside Shriya " Yes, actually, I am travelling solo."

Shantanu introduced himself to the new girl and asked her name. She said "Manjari" with a smile.

"Wow, nice name!" Rishabh was now attentive towards her.

"Do you smoke Manjari?" Shriya asked her noticing that Manjari had a pair of big light brown eyes that shone brightly even in the dim light.

"No, I don't." Manjari shifted her body in the chair.

"Hey Manjari, have you seen a ghost or a spirit?" Rishabh asked with a hint of mischief in his eyes.

"Why are you asking me this"? Manjari's face stiffened at the question.

"Areee it is nothing serious, it's just that our friend Rishabh here is totally obsessed with these topics and he would really like to see a ghost some day", Shantanu explained.

"Is that so? Well, no, I haven't seen a ghost but I know a lot of ghost stories that will blow your minds" Manjari's eyes were shining.

"Wow, come on then, tell us one story", Rishabh was intrigued.

"Yes tell him a very scary story, so that he stops talking about these things altogether" Shriya teased Rishabh.

Rishabh rolled his eyes at Shriya. Manjari was about to say something when Kaushik came on the terrace and joined the group. He sat on a chair beside Shantanu and asked them, how their evening was going. They all told him that their evening was going fabulous. Kaushik asked why was Neeti sitting on the swing by herself, Shantanu told him that she was scared of the topic that was going on in their conversations.

"Oh yes, I remember how she had panicked that day, she was really scared, still you all are talking about the same topic today!" Kaushik was the manager of the hostel, he was a friendly person and all the guests liked him because of his helpfulness and good humour.

They kept on talking about the weather and other random things for a little while, meanwhile, Rishabh was getting impatient to go back to his ghost story. He looked at Manjari who was not silently listening to everyone and she looked a little lost. Kaushik told them that he was going to sleep. He wished them good night and went to the swing to wish Neeti a good night too.

"Oh, Kaushik Bhaiya, you haven't slept yet, the night is very still today, isn't it?" Neeti took out her earplugs.

"Yeah, it is like that tonight. It is a little weird that there is no wind today and look at the lake water, it also seems very still, like something isn't right."

"Why are you scaring me, Kaushik Bhaiya? Please don't say such things, you know right I am still scared about that incident. I don't understand what happened to me, I had never been scared like that in my entire life."

"Okay, I will not say anything right now, maybe we can talk about this some other time, you know in daylight."

"Yes, that's right. Okay, now, I will also go to sleep. Are you going downstairs? I'll also come with you."

"Yes, I just wished everyone a good night, come, let's go."

Neeti got up and said, "Goodnight everyone, I am going to sleep, I will see you all tomorrow."

"Bye-bye, Goodnight, Sleep well, Don't be scared" were muttered.

After Kaushik and Neeti left, Manjari asked them why was Neeti sitting by herself and they told her that she was scared of the topics of ghosts and spirits lately.

Rishabh looked at Manjari excitedly and asked her to tell the story because he couldn't wait anymore.

Manjari started the story "Okay, I am going to start the story now but I don't want anyone to panic after I have finished the story."

No, No man and other similar words were muttered to assure Manjari that they are brave people who do not get afraid so easily. Manjari began telling the story "So once upon a time, there was a girl who lived with her Aunt in an old apartment. The apartment was situated in an old rusty building in a scarcely populated area. The girl and her Aunt had completely different personalities. The Aunt had a sweet personality, the girl had a bitter personality. The Aunt used to love animals and birds. She used to feed grains to the pigeons which used to come and sit on their balcony. The girl hated the sound of pigeons. The girl was frustrated with her life because she wanted to travel the world but her Psychiatrist had advised against it. The girl used to take out her frustration on random things.

One day the girl was hanging out by the balcony where pigeons used to sit and feed on the seeds. The girl kept glaring at the pigeons and tapping on the balcony to shoo them away but they continued to sit there. In the next moment, the girl extended her hand and grabbed one pigeon by its neck and in the next moment, the pigeon was lying down on the ground lifelessly. The aunt found out that the girl had killed the pigeon. She confronted the girl. The girl got furious and she pushed the aunt too off the balcony just like the pigeon. The next day three bodies were discovered, the pigeon, the aunt and can anyone guess whose body was the third one?"

Manjari looked at everyone to find questions on their faces. None of the friends uttered anything. All of them looked at Manjari to find answers. Manjari understood their questions and spoke further "The third body was of the girl because she couldn't live with the guilt of killing her favourite aunt so she took her own life, you know she was a troubled soul, it is said that their souls never found peace after their death, and to this day all three souls haunt that old flat in that old building."

Manjari sighed and looked at the sky and said, "Well, there are pigeons here all around too, right? I hope there isn't any girl here like the one in my story otherwise all of the town will be filled with the bodies of pigeons."

All the four friends were perplexed after hearing this. Rishabh said, "Well, yeah, but don't you think that it is a very strange story rather than a horror story?"

The others agreed with this. Shantanu said, "This story wouldn't have scared even Neeti."

All of them laughed loudly at this. Suddenly there was a group of birds which flew with a speed. Manjari looked at the sky with a little crooked smile and said,

"It is *Amavasya* tonight right? It is more fun to be somewhere on *Amavasya.*"

Shriya asked Manjari what did she mean by that, but Manjari didn't answer.

"Well it is 3:45 am already, I have to be somewhere else. There is another group of friends waiting for me" Saying this Manjari stood up and as she was about to leave, the friends were shocked upon hearing that she had to leave at that odd hour.

As Manjari was leaving, she turned to look at them with a wicked smile on her face and said "I never told you all the name of the girl in my story ,right ?"

The group looked at her curiously

"Her name was Manjari." The girl descended the stairs in a hurry.

"Wait, what?" Shriya shuddered in her seat and looked at her other friends.

"Man, she must be joking" Shantanu tried to logically explain it to Shriya.

"Yeah, we will ask her tomorrow when we see her", Rishabh tried to be practical.

"And also I will tell a very scary story to her then she will be the one to get scared " Faizal comforted Shriya and hugged her and Shriya laughed.

The next morning, Neeti came in a good mood in the common room and joined everyone for breakfast. Kaushik brought the bowl of cereal and handed it to Shantanu and asked,

"So for how long did you all sit there last night?"

Faizal answered while sipping his coffee "We left soon after Manjari finished telling her stupid story."

"Yeah" Shriya rolled her eyes.

"Who is Manjari?" asked Kaushik.

"*Areee*, the new girl who was sitting with us last night" Rishabh answered.

"Which girl?" Neeti asked this time.

"The girl who was dressed in a white t shirt and had long brownish hair and she was sitting next to Shriya" Shantanu said.

"I didn't see any girl" Neeti looked confused.

"Neither did I and there wasn't any new guest in the hostel yesterday" Kaushik looked at them with a worried expression.

"No, no, I know, you are trying to scare us, you have partnered up with Manjari" Rishabh tried to show his bravery.

"I swear Rishabh Bhaiya, there was no one on the terrace last night other than you guys" Kaushik tried to make them believe.

Shriya held Neeti's hand and asked her to swear on her mom's life that she didn't see Manjari sitting with them last night.

Neeti swore and told them that the chair next to Shriya was empty the entire time.

"Didn't you see her talking to us when you came and sat with us?" Rishabh was now agitated as he asked Kaushik.

"No Rishabh Bhaiya, when I was sitting there with you all, I did most of the talking and I didn't see any of you addressing anyone else other than you four" Kaushik was now bewildered too.

"Oh my God, she was in fact telling her own story" Shriya cupped her head with both of her hands. The faces of the other three also had lost their colour.

A VALLEY OF MAGIC

While hanging upside down from a tree with a thick wool rope in the middle of a forest, all Akhil could think of was that he should have learned how to respect women. Fate had brought him to the place called "*Jadde* Valley" but it was his own doing that he was currently in this condition.

Two days ago Akhil was roaming in the valley and he was just awestruck by the beauty of the place. "This valley is the most beautiful valley I have ever seen," he thought to himself while picking a beautiful white flower from the ground. The valley was situated in the Champa village in Uttarakhand. In the valley, a vast land was covered with all kinds of beautiful flowers. Akhil was travelling solo for the first time in his life. It was a new as well as strange experience for him.

Back home, when Akhil had told his friends that he was going on a solo trip, his friends had fed all sorts of nasty thoughts into his mind related to girls while travelling. He was sure to find a girl for himself on this trip. Being a guy who grew up completely devoid of female friendships, it didn't come naturally to him to talk to women.

On the first day of his stay in the traveller's hostel, he couldn't muster up the courage to initiate a conversation with the female travellers who were staying in the hostel. He had seen a couple of groups of friends hanging out in the common room and it made him regret his decision to come on a solo trip. He called his friend Sunny on the phone in the evening and told him what was going on there. Sunny tried to boost his confidence by telling him that he looks good and he is educated, and has a decent job, all he has to do is approach a woman and just make a random conversation and then things will work out eventually.

Sunny was telling the truth about Akhil being a good-looking guy. Being a *jaat,* he was well-built and his face was a mixture of innocence and sincerity. He was tall and if a person didn't talk to him and just looked at him from a distance, Akhil would appear like a decent guy.

The conversation with his friend had boosted Akhil's ego and he was in search of a suitable opportunity now. The following day, after breakfast, Akhil went for a walk on the narrow paths of the valley. A little cool breeze was blowing on his face and he was soaking up the beauty of the place when he saw a girl standing over a railing of the wall. He thought to himself that the girl is looking lonely, maybe she would appreciate some company. He approached the girl, cleared his throat and said " Hi, are you travelling solo too?"

The girl was startled as she didn't notice his presence before. She hesitated for a moment before speaking " Yes, I am."

She looked like she must have been in mid twenties. She had a round, chubby face with brown hair and she was wearing a black embroidered *kurti* with jeans. Akhil tried to initiate some more conversation but the girl was still hesitant in talking to him. Akhil asked her name, she said it was Suchi. Suchi started to leave from there abruptly. Akhil tried to ask her where she was headed but she paced quickly and turned towards the small parking space with quick movements.

Without giving it much thought, Akhil followed Suchi to the parking space where he saw her putting on her pink helmet and starting the ignition of her scooter.

Akhil too had parked his rented bike in the same space, he quickly reached for his bike and left right after Suchi. Suchi was riding her scooter at a normal speed and it was easier for Akhil to catch up to her. Suchi kept taking turns here and there and Akhil kept following her blindly. It was almost afternoon now. Suchi stopped her scooter outside a museum, and got down from her scooter. She opened the seat of her scooter, stored her helmet there, locked the scooter and entered the museum.

Akhil was determined to talk to Suchi now, so he again followed her inside the museum without realising that it was a big mistake he was making.

Inside the museum, Akhil saw Suchi standing in front of a painting of what looked like an old church. Suchi was quietly gazing at the painting when Akhil went and stood beside her. He said in a deep voice, “It looks mysterious and beautiful at the same time, isn't it?”

Once again Suchi was startled hearing a deep voice in the quiet museum. A mixed look of irritation and question passed on her face briefly before she nodded into a yes. Suchi wanted to ask Akhil what was he doing there, and did he follow her to the museum but she didn't ask.

Akhil was now more confident in talking to her. He asked Suchi where she was from and other things like that and Suchi answered them in a few words. Akhil was not able to recognise the hesitation in Suchi's answers. This went on for a while and after that, Suchi excused herself and said that she was leaving. Akhil was quick to catch up to her, he asked her where she was headed and Suchi told him that she was just going to roam around the valley. She put on her helmet and left on her scooter.

Akhil stood there, and thought for a moment before stalking Suchi one more time. She reached a small restaurant on the way to the *Jadde* valley where she parked her scooter and went inside. Akhil too parked his motorcycle and followed her inside the restaurant. It was a small restaurant made up of straws and clay and it looked like a hut from outside. Suchi went to the counter to place her order for tea and a sandwich. Akhil noticed her ordering the food. He ordered the same thing as Suchi.

Suchi had noticed Akhil but she pretended to not see him and quietly sat on a little table and ate her sandwich and drank her tea. Akhil was sitting on a chair in the opposite direction of Suchi. After finishing her food, Suchi again left one more time on her scooter. The only difference was that she was aware of Akhil following her this time. She kept checking out in the rear-view mirror of her scooter every now and then and each time Akhil was there on his motorcycle a few feet behind her.

Soon Suchi took to a secluded path that led to a forest area. The path was narrow and it was lined by wild trees. Now on the secluded road, only two people were there riding their bikes. One was Suchi and right behind her was Akhil. Akhil was thinking to himself why was Suchi headed on a secluded path like that and where was she actually going?

The sun was dimmer now given it was a winter day. In the mountains, the sunset is a very pleasant time. After a few minutes of riding, Suchi stopped her scooter near a big banyan tree. There was a well right beside the tree. The spot appeared unusual to Akhil. There weren't pretty and colourful flowers growing there like the ones he had seen in the valley on the first day. This place gave an eerie impression but Akhil tried to ignore it. While Akhil parked his motorcycle and gazed at the place, Suchi had disappeared behind a peepul tree. Akhil was still looking at the trees when his foot got stuck into something. It was a loop made of a rope. Before he could understand what was going on, he tipped over and in the next moment, he was hanging upside down from the banyan tree. Someone has set a trap in which he was trapped.

"Help, help!" Akhil started to shout but nobody came to his rescue. Now he started to take Suchi's name, he knew Suchi was there somewhere nearby and only she could save him now.

After a few moments, Suchi appeared from behind a mango tree but she wasn't alone. There were two more girls with her. One of them was very tall and she looked a bit younger than Suchi and the other one looked about the same age and she was short and slim. The three of the girls had sticks in their hands which were made out of tree branches. They had terrifying looks on their faces and none of them spoke a word. They all came near Akhil and circled him and started to take rounds and chant a mantra which was beyond Akhil's understanding.

Akhil was flabbergasted by all of this. He kept trying to talk to Suchi but it seemed to him like she was in a trance. She only kept looking at him with a constant scary expression. Akhil started to shout now, he began to apologise to her for stalking her and making her feel comfortable. He proceeded to swear that he wouldn't do anything like that ever in his life again. He swore that he would respect women and he would not listen to his idiot friends.

None of this seemed to work on any of the girls, the shorter girl suddenly kept her stick there and went from there. Suchi and the other girl also had stopped. Akhil thought that finally they had felt pity for him and they would him go now. The other girl came back with a lit candle in her hand. She placed it a few metres away from Akhil. The girl picked up her stick and the three of them again took one round and chanted the mantra. They dropped their sticks and looked at Akhil one more time before leaving together.

Now I leave it up to the readers to decide whether someone should rescue Akhil or not. Should Akhil be forgiven or punished for what he did?

THE FORGETFULNESS OF DARJI UNCLE

The *darji* *(tailor)* uncle works all the time. Whenever I reach there at his little shop, the shop which is made up of a sewing machine placed on a wooden table and some heaps of clothes waiting there to be altered, I always see him working on a piece of clothing. I reach there and ask him "Uncle, did you make my dress?" He looks up from the table, his black- rimmed square-shaped glasses dropped on his nose, and a look of realisation passes his face. He smiles sheepishly and in a meek voice he says, "Oh, no, I forgot about your dress."

I look at him with a fake angry expression and say in a fake angry voice "Uncle, didn't I tell you to make my dress by this evening?"

He again smiles a little smile and explains to me how he took out the piece of clothing I had given to him three days ago to work on, but a customer of his came and demanded that he alter her dress right away. He says that the lady wouldn't leave so he had to make her dress first and mine was forgotten. He promises me that he will alter my *kurti* by eight o'clock tonight.

When I reach again at nine o'clock this time, he again has forgotten about my dress. I give him a final time and a stricter reminder to make my dress on time because I have to catch a flight tomorrow. He tells me that he will hundred per cent alter the dress on time. This happens all the time but the question is why do I keep going to the same *darji* uncle all the time? Why don't I find another *darji* uncle who can deliver on time? Well, the answer is that my *darji* uncle is an honest and hardworking person and he is proficient at his work. He alters the clothes perfectly and never overcharges me for any of the work. If he wanted, he could ask me for more money for the alterations and I wouldn't be able to deny him. When it comes to negotiations and bargaining, I am as good as a newborn baby being able to tell why it is crying. One time *darji* uncle had gone to his village for a month. I needed an urgent alteration done on my newly bought magenta-coloured anarkali kurta, so I went up to another darji uncle who sits in the Meena market.

I gave the new darji uncle the piece of clothing, told him I would be back to collect it by seven o'clock the same evening. That darji uncle called me at six o'clock and told me that my kurta was ready. When I went there to collect the kurta, that darji uncle asked me to pay a much-exaggerated price for that not-so-elaborated work. I paid him the money anyway because I didn't want to argue. Upon reaching home, I tried the outfit on, it was shorter in the front and longer in the back and no it can't be corrected by altering it more. It is needless to say the magenta anarkali kurta is resting at the back of my closet with other discarded clothes.

One day when I reached around the corner of the street where *my darji* uncle has set up his little shop, I saw a small crowd gathered there. Some of those people were shouting but I couldn't figure out what were they saying from a distance. A few people were standing on the other side of the road and they were watching whatever was happening with a keen interest. After I got closer, I saw a man holding the collar of Darji uncle's shirt in his hands. Darji Uncle was looking terrified, he had a few scratches on his arms. I could see in his small spectacle-covered eyes that he was about to cry any minute.

A plus-sized lady wearing a blue ankle-len gth dress was repeatedly asking him "Tell me, where have you hidden it, tell me?" She even uttered a few curse words and that made me lose my cool. I asked the people to move a bit aside and I moved closer to Darji Uncle. He looked at me with pleading eyes. I asked the screaming lady what was happening. She told me that her gold ring was lost which she claimed that she had kept inside the pocket of her black dress. Three days ago she had given the same dress to Darji uncle to alter. She was asking him to give the ring back but the "bloody thief" wasn't giving it back. While addressing the crowd, she said that it was her engagement ring which her husband had given to her ten years ago.

I turned to Darji uncle and asked him if he had seen the ring inside the pocket of the dress. He shook his head in no with tear-filled eyes and I knew he was telling the truth. I asked the blood-red-eyed man to let go of the collar of Darji uncle's shirt. He did it unwillingly. Now I turned towards the lady whose swollen face had gotten red with anger and asked her to calm down. Instead of calming down, the lady was more agitated now because I told her that Darji Uncle is an honest and hardworking man and he can't be a thief.

The lady and the man had started to threaten Darji Uncle by saying that they would call the cops on him. Darji Uncle got scared because he couldn't risk to getting into police trouble. I tried to make the lady understand but she was in no mood to listen. When they didn't calm down, I asked the lady how much her gold ring cost. She said that it cost her around fifteen thousand rupees. Listening to fifteen thousand rupees, Darji uncle was flabbergasted. He started to fidget around in the drawer of his sewing machine table. I asked him what was he doing, he told me frantically that he was looking for money to give to the lady. Before I could say something, Darji uncle had gathered a bunch of five hundred rupee notes and gave it to the lady. The lady almost grabbed the cash from his hands and gave it to the man who was with her. The man shot a nasty look towards Darji uncle before beginning to count the money. After he was finished counting, he said it was only five thousand and five hundred rupees. The swollen-faced lady once again began screaming.

Darji uncle stood there with his hands folded. I knew the lady and the man wouldn't leave until they had fifteen thousand rupees in their hands. I talked to them and transferred the rest of the nine thousand and five hundred rupees online into their bank account. They were satisfied when they left a tired and sad Darji uncle behind. The crowd also dispersed slowly. Darji uncle was saying thank you to me again and again which I couldn't bear so I came back home after giving him the pair of trousers to alter. He had altered my trousers the same evening.

A week later, I received a surprising call from Darji uncle's number. He had called me to his shop, said he had an urgent business with me. I went there to find him his little smile back on his face. I asked him what was the matter, he told me to take a seat on the plastic chair beside him. I sat there quietly. He took out a bundle of cash from the drawer of his little work table. I expressed my surprise and I tried to tell him that he didn't need to give me the money back so soon, I knew how hard he worked to make money. But he told me something next which made me take the money.

Darji uncle told me that he had found the lady's gold ring in another dress's layers while he was altering that. He said that he was in a hurry to alter the dress and the ring must have fallen from the pocket of the lady's dress and would have gotten jumbled up in the layers of another dress. I asked him how he didn't notice the ring falling to which he replied that he had seen a glimpse of a shiny thing but thought of it as a button and then later forgot to check what it was. That day when the lady and the man left after taking the money, he had checked everywhere, inside every plastic bag and then he found the ring in one of the dresses.

I asked him did the couple easily return the money after getting the ring back, to which he replied that he didn't return their ring. He had sold the gold ring and he had gotten fourteen thousand rupees after selling it. I was shocked to know that a nice man like Darji uncle could do something like that. He smiled one of his unusual smiles and said that if the lady and the man had been nicer to him,

he would have returned their ring. But despite being a regular customer for all these years, the lady didn't have the decency to handle the situation gracefully, so why should he show grace to those people? I agreed.

ABOUT THE AUTHOR

Nipram Pankhuri is an emerging author with a strong academic background in Psychology. Since her childhood, Nipram has been fascinated with the world of fiction, she was very fond of reading stories even as a child. Her mother was also a short story writer and that inspired Nipram to dwell into the world of fiction writing. While she decided to pursue her career in Psychology, it was writing that intrigued her more. She decided to write about her experiences of traveling with the touch of imagination and turn it into a collection of short stories.

Verses Kindler Publication

Verses Kindler Publication

Reach us through our website -

https://www.verseskindlerpublication.com/

For more information, visit our

Instagram or Facebook page.